Catnip Gray
The Tabitha D

by
Charles Harvey

* * * * *

PUBLISHED BY:
Wes Writers and Publishers @ Amazon

Catnip Gray Cat Detective
The Tabitha Davenport Affair

****

Disclaimer

This is a work of fiction. The names, characters, places, and incidents are products of the writer's imagination and are not to be construed as real. Any resemblance to persons, living or dead, actual events, organizations, or locales is entirely coincidental.

Please subscribe to the mailing list for exciting updates. Thank you. **Subscribe**
http://forms.aweber.com/form/52/1200451752.htm

Author's Website www.charlesharveyauthor.com

Table of Contents

Chapter 1-Slim-Fast High

The day began like any other, with me yawning at the yellow sun. It was noon. I was halfway into a long stretch when someone bumped my cat door. Actually, it's a doggy door that I had converted for cats only.

"What's the difference?" you ask.

"The difference is the difference," I say. Plus the mural painted on the flap showing a Cantonese family enjoying a Pomeranian for supper sends a strong message to the pooches.

"Come in," I meowed in a gruff Slim-Fast soaked voiced. The night before had been long and adventurous with me jumping from tabletop to couch, on top of the china cabinet, to the end table whereupon I shook my tail and made a pair of fish-shaped Tiffany vases tremble. The pair presenting such a cool blue steely facade amongst the common bric-a-brac and Norman Rockwell plates, shook as my tail swept their elegant bodies. They were the kind of vases meant to be looked at and to prove their owners, the Grays, were about something. However, I know their brains were screaming for a Valium and a martini. I'm sure they recalled the days when they were a trio bopping to jazz music blasting from the hi-fi. Yes there once had been three of them. Memories are like shattered glass. Feet never forget the shards that done them in.

After all of that romping, I had hit this bar called the Kitchen Floor and quenched my thirst with a nightcap of

Slim-Fast. Of course, it didn't stop with one saucer--never does. I go on mewling for more and slurping saucer after saucer of the stuff as I foolishly try to drown my memories. But memories can't be drowned. Reflected in the shiny steel door of the Kitchen Floor's refrigerator, I saw her. But like a mirage, she vanished. I remembered Electra was dead. The recollection cut like a knife across my tail and drove me to consume saucer after saucer of Slim-Fast until I could remember no more. I had no memory of getting home or anything until my cat door thumped and woke me up in the middle of the smiling yellow noonday sun.

"Come in," I meowed a second time.

She sauntered in dressed in black fur and white boots. I thought this was an odd way to be clothed in July, until I caught a glimpse of my twitching tail, and remembered fur was the clothing option for all cats, except those hairless, wrinkled species among us who look like nude senior citizens. My eye caught the ruby and diamond necklace dangling from her neck.

"Dame is loaded," I said to myself.

She sauntered around the room, sniffed at the scratched up divan, and turned her nose up. She sat and her thick tail swept the air like a hand dismissing an irritating child. Her tail brushed the floor and sent a Slim-Fast cap under the couch. If the clattering noise startled her, she didn't react. Her green eyes bore into me as I sat nibbling my paw. I had calmed down after jumping straight up, taking a defensive stance and landing nose to the floor and butt in the air. That Slim-Fast bottle cap had set my nerves on edge.

"Maybe you're not the cat for the job," she purred and looked out the window.

Just then the cuckoo clock on the fireplace mantle struck three times as it always does on the hour no matter the time of day or night. She took no notice of the blue cuckoo. I quashed my urge to pounce upon it as I did when no one was around.

"She already thinks I'm a fool," I said to myself.

"How can I help you Miss...um...?"

"You'll know me as Tabitha Davenport."

"But not the real you?"

"Tabitha Davenport is all you need to know."

"Rex Gray is the name. All my friends call me Catnip Gray." I held out my paw. She nodded her head.

"I don't trust *friends*."

"I am a Private Investigator."

"I discerned as much from the faint orange neon sign glowing in the window. It was a choice between your sign and the well lettered blue one in the window next door. I admit I did look in that window, but there appeared to be no one about."

"I'm glad my reputation brought you to me," I said sarcastically.

"You don't have to be as brilliant as Sherlock Holmes. Being adequate is all I require of you, Mister Catnip Gray. And being courteous."

I shrugged and offered her a pinch of catnip. Her pupils brightened for a moment, but she quickly caught herself and turned her nose up at it. I decided against any myself. Me suddenly sprinting after my shadow would have confirmed to her that she should have gone next door to Sneaky Sam's Detective Agency and waited for his return. Of course, waiting would have done her no good. This was the day for his vet appointment. I imagined at this moment a woman's warm fingers were expressing his glands.

"How can I help you today, Tabby?"

The look she gave me could have melted a frozen turkey. "I'm not at all familiar with you, Sir."

"Excuse me, Miss Davenport."

"Misses Tabitha Davenport."

She whipped a photo out of her purse--your usual wedding photo of a couple about to cut into their wedding fish cakes. The groom was white--all white with pink eyes. "Albino, snow leopard, white snake," I thought to myself. He wore a black bowtie. His red cummerbund resembled a bloody slash across his chest. A diamond tiara sat crooked on Tabitha's head. Her face was veiled in white chiffon. He grinned like a Cheshire as she smiled standing next to him.

"Friend of yours?" I joked.

She sighed, rolled her eyes toward the ceiling, blinked, and looked off into the distance. I felt like a fool.

"Of course, he's your husband."

"Will be ex-husband if you do your job right." Tabitha gave me a photo of another feline. The broad in this picture was all gray except for the black stripes above her eyes, which gave her a devilish persona. An emerald green choker decorated with gaudy rhinestones ringed her neck. She posed in the picture window of a little box-shaped apartment surrounded by other boxy dens. The management of these caves thought they were clever in painting the units hues of orange, yellow, lime, and strawberry. Each unit had a black door. At dusk, this ghetto resembled a mess of flies trapped in sherbet. I knew the compound well. Lots of single felines call it home. I've done some tomcatting at the Cubbyhole Arms myself on more than one occasion.

"Her name is Dorothy Green," Tabitha hissed. "She lives in those common apartments on Tuna Boulevard. I want my husband and her photographed together."

"Easy as pie. I'll photo-shop this wedding picture--replace your mug with hers."

Tabitha broke down sobbing. "You're a cruel fool, Mr. Catnip Gray. I should not have come here." She made for the door. I caught up with her just as her nose was about to push it open.

"I'm sorry. I'm sorry," I said over and over. It had started to rain. She changed her mind about leaving, turned and sat down.

"That's exactly what she wants to do to me--cut me out of my marriage. I think she's trying to have me killed." She dabbed her eyes with a silk hanky.

"You should go to the cops."

"You can't take suspicions to the police. I already tried anyway. All they did was pat my head and offer me a can of cheap tuna as if I was some kind of homeless stray. I've come to you Mr. Catnip because I have no one else to turn to. I need hard evidence of them together--something that will stand up in Divorce Court."

She didn't wince when I told her my fee. Ten sardines a day plus expenses--five today as a deposit. She paid the deposit and promised the rest when I had the photo.

This job is too easy, I said as I peered through the Venetian blinds at her swaying hips shimmying from side to side. I knew the layout of the Cubbyhole Apartments. How hard can it be to spot an albino cat? I could do this job in a night. But I wanted to milk her for at least a week. I needed fifty sardines. Rent was due on the office. My Slim-Fast habit was taking a bite out of my bank account.

Tabitha Davenport stopped at the edge of a flower patch. Suddenly her whole body lurched forward. I heard a loud hacking as if she was being choked. She heaved up something greenish, stood looking at the mess for a moment, and walked on. "I'm glad she didn't leave that in here," I thought to myself as I watched her approach a red Jaguar. The door opened and she hopped in. The car eased into traffic quiet and stealthily, as any dignified cat should.

I jumped on the counter and peered into my cupboard. No Slim-Fast. I looked at the trashcan. Slim-Fast bottles spilled from its gaping jaw onto the floor. I needed a fix bad. The fools who run this joint I call home wouldn't be arriving from their jobs for another five hours. This Slim-Fast business started out as her kick to lose weight. She had opened a bottle and was drinking so fast chocolate dribbled down her chin. He came into the kitchen and called her a slobbering cow. The fight was on. The Slim-Fast bottle was thrown landing on the linoleum spilling its contents onto the waxed daisies. I licked and got hooked. I'm reduced to rubbing my body against her fat ankles to get my fix while the bar is closed during the day. Oh, so ignoble for a cat to be at the mercy of a bad habit. But I needed a fix. I couldn't wait for that fool to get home. I'd have to slip over the old folks home and trick some doddering dame out of a saucer of that hideous Ensure. A cat's gotta do what a fish won't do. That's my favorite saying. It means what it means.

****

I belong to the Grays a very weird and strangely strange couple. They both could use a lot more fur. The woman has more atop her head. It changes a different color almost every Friday evening. Sometimes it's gold, sometimes ruby-red. She's even tried blue and lime green and combinations too hideous to mention. Most of the time her efforts end in copious amounts of tears and curse words. The man? He has a bald spot between his jungle bush hairs. It looks alike a saucer of milk. I climbed up the back of the chair and tried to lick it one day. It doesn't taste like either milk or Slim-Fast. I detected a minty odor like in the gum he sticks under the dining table. Yes they need more hair. The furry patch in the middle of their bodies is not enough.

The house we live in has many rooms inside of it. One large room is really all they need. It's senseless to me to have a separate room to eat and a separate room to sleep, and a separate room to sit and watch that picture-box thing. One room with a litter box pushed in the corner is all they need. Well that's enough for me. But I do prefer the front room with the picture-box thing. It has a large window from which I can see the whole world. That world is far more interesting than anything I see on the picture-box.

The woman spends every Saturday running a loud machine over the rugs. I haven't the slightest idea of the story behind that activity. But she seems to take keen joy in it, especially while the man is watching other men on the picture-box in tight pants running into each other. The machine makes me nervous to the point, I climb up the curtains until she's done. Afterwards, a nice hairball expelled from my gut soothes my nerves, but starts her to screeching at the op of her lungs. I ignore her screeching. I think it's meant for him anyway.

The kitchen is my next favorite room. Besides that hideous dry stuff they feed me, that where they keep the Slim-Fast. The kitchen is also the room where the man and woman do most of their fussing in the kitchen. All he has to do is open his trap and go, "What's for dinner?" Her face steams red as she stirs a bubbling pot of something greenish. She screeches and he bellows. Sounds like *The Animal Kingdom* in there. After a moment, she runs to the bedroom and slams the door. He grabs a beer, some pepperoni, and sits in front of the picture box. He seems more happier than when he eats the green stuff. However things go nuts if she runs into the bathroom. World war breaks out.

"I'm going to shit right in this pot if you don't come out of there, Diane!"

"Go ahead you bastard (I think that his name), you can eat it for all I care."

"It'll taste a lot better than anyone you cook," he says turning up the volume on the picture-box. In a moment the house turns black. The picture book glows blue before turning black. You can hear toilets flushing three doors down and doves cooing. Diane has turned off the electricity. Depending on how much beer he's consumed, he'll either kick the door, or fall down on his knees, and croon into the doorknob. "Please, baby, please. Turn the lights on. I love your kale and black bean soup. I love you, baby. You know what else I love?"

"What?"

"I love you custard pudding. I love how you smear it all over you."

By this time I'm ready to hack up another hairball. Too much drama. He'd save himself a lot of grief and door repairs, if he'd learn to get down on his knees and rub her ankles at suppertime and just accept whatever she dishes out. She and I never argue about food.

They have no children yet—thank god. However, something they call a niece comes over and likes to carry me around in her arms like I'm a Raggedy Ann doll.

"Aw, so cute," they coo. Just wait until I scratch those fat arms. Then who's going to be cute?

Chapter 2 -Recollections

On my way out later that evening, I passed the spot where Tabitha had hacked up her hairball and noticed it was clean, except for a strand of white hair in the grass and a crumb of Meow Mix. "Scavengers about," I said to myself. "Perhaps a hungry dog." As I sharpened my claws and twitched my tail, my nose didn't pick up any canine scent. But I did smell a rat. I noted a bite mark on a blade of grass near the long gone hairball--an enormous bite mark, sharp and triangular. There's only one creature who has teeth like that, and that's Ace the Rat--Detective Ace he preferred. However, we legit Private eyes just called him Rat. He gathered information by nosing around sewers and dumpsters, something no respectable cat would be caught doing. Plus he ate as much evidence as he gleaned. But why would Rat be nosing around Cat Alley? Cat Alley where I live is a tough place even for robust cats like me. It's a concrete jungle of stray hoodlums running around with parts of ears and tails bitten off from turf wars, acting as if being maimed is a badge of honor. They'll steal the stink out of cat litter if you let 'em. Lucky they were all asleep when Tabitha was here. I can just picture them mugging her for her fine collar or the stacks of sardines she carried in her purse. A rat doesn't stand a chance in Cat Alley. But yet Ace was here. Could he have been following her? She did mention she thought her husband and his mistress were out to get her.

A fly buzzed near the hairball spot. I swatted at it a few times before I brought it down. I picked it up, tossed it in the air, and swallowed it. I then spit it out along with my own whopper of a healthy hairball. If Ace were still around, this would be a good way to trap him and see what he was up to. He'd be drawn to the hairball. I forgot about visiting the old folks at Sunset Arms and went back to my office. Lady Luck shined on me. A half full bottle of Slim-Fast sat on the fireplace mantle beneath the cuckoo clock. The woman had left it two days ago to answer the phone. I sniffed. The rich chocolate aroma tickled my whiskers. It was still good. I knocked the bottle from the fireplace and prayed it would land on the clean white linoleum and not the wooly carpet. My aim was good and chocolaty Slim-Fast formed a Rorschach pattern depicting a bird eating a squirrel. I lapped and batted the bottle around a bit. In a moment, I grew tired of this strenuous activity and jumped onto the windowsill to watch for Ace. I waited. I snoozed. I snoozed. I waited. I snoozed with one eye open. No Ace.

The mailman sauntered into the courtyard. A dog across the yard raised a stink—pawing and growling while his snout poked through the blinds. He saw me staring at him and grew emboldened. This is the same pooch who took a member of the Alley Cats for an involuntary ride on his back. The postman put a few letters and postcards in our mail slot. I jumped down and nosed around the postcards. Postcards mean trouble. It's the primary means of communication from the Vet. I make sure all postcards make it to my litter box—including the one from Diane's fowl smelling great Aunt Tillie. I leave the letters with the little windows intact. Those always seem to bring on more screeching and door slamming.

Later that night after supper and as the Grays hissed at each other over a couple of the windowed envelopes, I decided to saunter over to the Cubbyhole Arms and see what I could see. Tuna Boulevard was three blocks over. It was a wide four-lane sea of concrete where cars whizzed by like lemmings. Many a life was lost under the wheels of Thunderbirds, Mustangs, Cobras, cougars, jaguars, and other monstrous beasts that humans drive. That's how Electra died.

We had just left Fred's Place--a little hole in the wall where the catnip and rare salmon liquor is freely passed around under the haunting voice of Black Bella mewing softly from the blue-lighted stage:

Meow meow meow
My Tom done gone
got himself a new
catfish bone
Meow meow meow
I'm so all alone
Oh willow, weep for me

Electra and I had swooned under the influence of the intoxicating air. After Fred's closed, we were a frisky pair hopping over trash cans, leaping up on fences, peering into windows, and laughing at human's silly attempts at lovemaking. We'd scream insults through the glass. "Really dude, more hair on your butt would drive her wild...Bite her ear you fool! Stop talking. More yowling ...You call that thing a tail?"

We scampered off when a naked bear looking man threw a house slipper at us. As we approached Tuna Boulevard, Electra suddenly darted out and an old sixty-seven Falcon sped up and sent her tumbling into a rosebush. It wrenched my heart watching my lover in death's bittersweet clutches as the rose's thorns pierced her flesh and teased me with their red petals and seductive scents. Roses were me and Electra's favorite flower to paw and nibble. I vowed to avenge Electra's death one day.

So as I stood at the edge of Tuna Boulevard, I got my eyes out for a yellow Falcon. Been watching for it for a year--waiting for my chance. I had all of my parakeets lined up in a row. The Falcon has a vinyl top. A crow told me he and his flock love splattering that top with a potent brand of bird poo. "It's old and soft as dog guts," the crow cawed. My plan called for me to sink my claws deep into that vinyl top and cause a lot of havoc.

I put one paw forward and stepped into the gutter when my ears picked up the whine of an old V8 motor. It sounded like a monkey with his tail caught in a meat grinder screaming a long, painful, "Eeeeeeee!" The guys at the Rat Trap Mechanic Shop said the noise meant loose belts, but the Falcon's fool owner likened the disquietude to a scream of death. He experienced many moments of perverse joy as he struck fear into the hearts of dogs, cats, and a few humans as he raced the falcon towards their poor souls. That Falcon had to be stopped.

I had gone over my plans in my head many times. Like a general plotting war strategy, I'd made crude mock-ups of scenarios using chicken bones and discarded Slim-Fast bottle caps. I pawed through a few pages of Diane's old High school Geometry and Algebra textbooks. Most of everything in life depends on an angle. *"Train X and train Y had to meet at noon in Kansas when they left their respective stations in New York and Los Angeles. How fast did each train have to travel?"* What did that have to do with me catching the Falcon? Nothing and everything. I had my angle down pat. I'd make my move when I saw those hideous yellowish headlights rush toward the lamppost. They had to strike the post at a perfect forty-five-degree angle as the Falcon traveled thirty-eight miles per hour. I waited.

When the car rounded Tuna Boulevard's ass shaped curve and the headlights struck the pole at its aforementioned angle, I leapt into the street. As I expected, the motor gunned. The falcon saw me. The concrete vibrated as he roared toward me. Acrid oil smoke filled my lungs. As the Falcon sped toward the bus stop, I started counting. On the count of ten, I leaped into the air and landed flat on the windshield. My claws gripped the edge of the vinyl top. Gravity flattened my body as if all of my bones had melted. My furry body obscured his view. He weaved the car from side to side like a punch-drunk boxer. The windshield wipers turned on. The blade on the driver's side hit my foot. I kicked and it straightened like a Conductor's baton, going round and around as if playing the same musical note over and over. I glimpsed the mad fool behind the falcon's wheel. His eyes bulged and he slobbered like a rabid dog as he tried to maneuver his head around my body. Something snapped under the Falcon's hood. The engine smoked. The mad fool turned the Falcon's wheel left and right, but the Falcon stayed on a straight course. Suddenly I felt heat on my back. I heard what sounded like a hundred geese honking. I knew it was an International Eagle eighteen-wheeler. My instinct told me the mad fool couldn't turn the Falcon's steering wheel and that we were headed straight for the truck. I knew I was doomed if I didn't act quickly. I had only seconds. Overhead tree branches hung low. I had to take a chance. I leaped up and clawed at the leaves. I prayed there would be a solid branch for me to hug or else I was going to fall back on the Falcon's roof or the busy street below. Miss Serendipity was with me as always as my nine lives ticked away one at a time. My arms and legs found a branch and I hung on tight. An explosion shook the tree, but I stayed put. I looked down and the falcon's nose was wedged into the International Eagle's grill. Picture a snake with a rat trapped in its jaws. I noticed a sparrow perched next to me startled to deathly stillness.

How lucky I am to have so many lives, I said to myself as I brushed some feathers from my mouth and continued down the sidewalk toward the Cubbyhole Arms. Sirens wailed behind me like hundreds of yowling cats. Foolish dogs howled in grief.

****

I slipped through the Cubbyhole Arm's gate. My keen detective senses told me to avoid windows with bright lights. Bright lights are not the settings of romantic interludes. I looked for lights that painted rooms in shades of umber, mauve, or shades of gray. The near darkness is where my whiskers are most potent. Windows were of no use either if they were shut. My whiskers cannot penetrate a closed off world.

I peered into a dozen half lit windows. The most I saw were humans doing strange things to each other or watching porn on their computer boxes. I watched as they twisted and contorted their bodies in their clumsy attempts at sex. I listened to them groaning and moaning like beasts in the bellies of beasts. I observed them salivating over salacious scenes of Internet sickness. I felt sick and disgusted. In another window, a dog saw me and growled until his master came and boxed him on the ears. I sprayed the window thoroughly with cat piss. Now he would have my smell to go along with his hurt head, lest he forgets the next day. A dog's memory is not worth spit in a hurricane.

Two windows over, a lovely feline gave herself a bath. Starting with her face, she dabbed her cute pink nose with her powdery white paw. She slowly licked her paw and combed it over her long blonde hair. I followed her rose colored tongue as she flicked it across her chest, easing inch by inch to her belly. She raised one leg and swept that tongue from hip to toe. My tail switched back and forth and rustled the leaves. She stopped and looked in my direction. I ducked behind a shutter. With her eyes half closed, she continued her exhibition. Her leg went higher and her tongue swept over her thigh to the center of her honeypot. She licked seductively. My heart went wild. My own tongue hung from my mouth as if I was being choked. The feline raised her other leg. It was the color of a dark silk stocking. I watched with anticipation until a large Bull Mastiff appeared in the window and barked. I fell off my perch and landed in a box of petunias two stories below.

I lay stunned for a moment until the wind rustled a petunia making it tickle my ear. As the haze lifted from my eyes and I shook myself, I realized I was in front of a large picture window in a well-lighted room. Three cats frolicked. My eyes popped open. I instantly recognized Tabitha Davenport by her white boots. She wore nothing else. The other feline dressed in a gray leotard and a dark green mask, I surmised to be Dorothy Green. She held a long leather strap in her teeth. She whipped it around the room and brought it down with a snap. The other cat in the room--all white, a translucent-white with one pink eye covered with an eye-patch, waved his paw around and appeared to be directing the two felines. He could be none other than Bill Davenport. I looked over to the right of them and a camera sat atop a tripod. The blinking red light indicated the whole sordid affair was being recorded. Davenport flicked his tail and Dorothy raised the whip and lashed it to the floor close to Tabitha's twitching tail. He took a sip of milk from a champagne glass and winked. Both felines moved and snuggled against him. Tiny plastic bags of catnip spilled their contents all over the floor around them. It was indeed a drug and sex orgy.

"What the devil," I wondered aloud. Suddenly all three of them pounced on a ball of silk yarn, unraveling the sensuous ribbon over their bodies. They slapped each other's tails, arched their backs and nibbled each other ears. At times, they would stop and glance at the television. On the TV screen, young kittens frolicked innocently, unwittingly arousing the prurient interest of adult cats. "Kitty porn" I gasped. Each glance at the visage of young kittens drove the trio to a high frenzy and they continued in greater excess their own activities. Davenport dragged from under the couch a huge hambone fit only for a Doberman or Boxer to ravish. He nodded and the felines straddled and rubbed their bellies up and down the bone.

When they grew bored with this activity, they climbed a long rope with a silk tassel tangling at the end. Davenport lay under the tassel on his back with his legs and arms wide open. The two felines swung and gyrated their bodies forcing the tassel to sweep across Davenport's lower body. His lips trembled as he mewed with debaucherous pleasure. I watched his tail sweep the floor keeping in rhythm to the teasing tassel. He then turned over and arched his back and tail so that the tassel powered by the swinging felines, swept over his lower back. He shut his eyes and shuddered and twitched. He then grew still and appeared to be snoozing. The vixens hanging onto the rope weren't ready for the fun to end. They swept their tails into the catnip and dusted Davenport's face. For their "naughtiness" he picked up the leather string and cracked it at their backsides. They scampered around the room meowing and clawing at the furnishings. Davenport grabbed both felines and held them down. He licked behind their ears as they mewed and shuddered in an orgasmic frenzy. Then, they lay panting and spent, tangled into each other and fell asleep.

As I climbed down from my perch, I spotted a long black tail disappearing under a pile of leaves. I pounced, but my claws struck a frog's tough hide. He leaped into the air, croaked, and hopped away. I was frightened senseless.

Chapter 3 -The Puzzle

Tabitha Davenport sat perched on a little stool in front of my desk. She watched me take a sip of Slim-Fast. I watched her watch me. The cuckoo clock struck three times. I paid no attention to the bird. I focused my whole being on this feline. She sighed and nibbled her nails.

"So, Mr. Catnip, have you made any progress in obtaining the photo of Dorothy Green and my husband?"

"These things take time."

"How much time, Mr. Catnip? He goes out philandering every night. I've followed him myself to the Cubbyhole Arms."

"Then why haven't you taken the picture?"

Tabitha stopped nibbling her nails. She stared at me for a moment before looking away.

"I'm such a complicated feline. I know what Bill is doing. I see her gray hairs all over his tail and cheek. I know what despicable acts they've committed, but I can't bear to record them myself. I need the shield of a photograph taken by someone else, a kind of emotional barrier--a shield to spare my heart."

I looked past her crying eyes and at the red choker around her neck. It was the one she wore the night I watched them frolicking. My cellphone rang. I answered it and excused myself. I lied it was a personal call I had to take in private. It was just a ruse I used to go outside and get a closer look at the Jaguar that had ferried her to my office.

As the telemarketer prattled on about the virtues of Golden Oaks Burial Policies, I sauntered up to the car. I retrieved a little vial of catnip from my pocket and took a sniff. It aroused my senses, especially my manhood. I raised my tail and marked each tire with a strong spray. As I rounded the back of the Jag, I saw something brush against the rear window. I casually strolled down the sidewalk toward my office. Then as if struck by lightning, I dove into some bushes and scampered up a nearby tree. I crept over a limb placing me a few feet from the car's window. Leaves hid my face. In the window, a huge white cat dozed. He had the dazzling white almost translucent coat of Bill Davenport, the man with his arm around Tabitha's shoulders in her wedding picture--the man who directed Tabitha and Dorothy in that sordid video. What the devil now, I wondered to myself. Curiosity balled up in my belly and I hacked a hairball clear across the courtyard. When I descended from the tree, the spot where the hairball should have landed was clean as a pigeon's tooth. I knew what that meant. Leaves rustled in the distance. Ace the Rat had struck again--that smelly hairball-eating rat!

"Perhaps this will help you get closer to my husband and Dorothy Green," Tabitha said when I returned to my office. She retrieved a small fish-shaped vessel from her purse. The tail was flat allowing the jar to stand up. A cork plugged in the mouth served as a stopper. The bottle resembled a foolish looking trout caught at the end of a fishing pole. I knew it wasn't a real fish, but I sniffed it anyway.

"Deliver this to Dorothy tonight at eleven p.m." Tabitha continued. "She will be expecting you. I will ring her telephone and tell her to expect a free tuna pizza from the Fish Gut Café. She's foolish and cheap and a sucker for anything free. My husband will be there, but will probably hide when he hears your knock. He's funny that way. He runs under the bed when he hears a knock at the door. When you open this jar, the aroma will draw him out, make him purr and rub against Dorothy. You snap their picture and I'll have my divorce and half of his millions of sardines."

She handed me the jar. I sniffed and toyed with the cork stopper. Tabitha wagged her paw and stopped me.

"Tut, tut, Mr. Catnip. If you open it too soon, the aroma will be too weak to draw Bill into the room. Wait until Dorothy opens her filthy door."

As she got ready to leave, Tabitha toyed with a piece of ribbon on my desk. "I'll be a very rich woman, Mr. Catnip--a lonely rich woman." Tabitha dangled a sardine in front of my nose and dropped it into a dish on my desk. She wrapped one end of the ribbon around my neck, turned and brushed her fluffy tail across my face. My tail rose along with all of my Tomcat instinct. I wanted her right then and there. She was a bad feline--full of feline wiles and lies. I watched her tail twitch seductively as she walked out the door and down the walkway. The door to the Jaguar opened and she hopped in. When the car turned, I saw in the back window Tabitha lying next to her husband. They playfully bit each other's tails.

Truth hides deep in a pack of lies waiting to be peeled like an onion, one layer at a time. I don't like onions, but I do love the truth. That's why I'm a private eye. Folks don't hire me to tell them lies. Folks hire me to find the truth. In the muck and cesspool of life, we want the truth as clean and shiny as a cat's eye marble. "What's my rascal of a husband up to? Who stole Aunt Jane's jewels? Who's buried in Grant's tomb? Who killed my golden goose? Why did the chicken cross the super highway?" Well, you get my drift. I don't take kindly to anyone trying to pull the dog's fur over my eyes. This dame Tabitha doesn't want the truth. I need to find out why.

Later that night, I decided to take a stroll. I knew I was supposed to deliver the jar to Dorothy Green at eleven; however my cat curiosity led me to do otherwise. I left it on my desk. I passed the spot where the Jaguar had been parked and picked up my scent. I expected my nose would take me to the Cubbyhole Arms and it did. I looked up at apartment number Four-one-one. The windows were black.

I spotted the Jaguar parked next to a broken down Phoenix. I was disappointed. I had hoped to follow its trail beyond the Cubbyhole Arms to a particular mansion in the Exclusive Persian Estates. I know that's where fat cats reside like Bill and Tabitha reside. The Cubbyhole Arms was only a place for them to slum. I hopped onto the hood of the Phoenix and peered into the Jaguar's windows. The white leather seats gleamed immaculately. Not a strand of cat fur to be seen anywhere. A pair of white gloves lay crumpled across the dashboard. They probably belong to the driver, I reasoned. The center console and dash were made of real scratchable wood that I ached to sink my claws into. An object between the seats caught my eye. I jumped from the Phoenix to the Jaguar's hood. A jar exactly like the one Tabitha asked me to deliver to Dorothy was jammed between the bucket seats. However, there was one minor detail, the jar in the Jag was embossed in red with a skull and crossbones. Poison.

An owl hooted. I looked up in a tree and saw its large yellow eyes. As I scanned the branches, I caught sight of a pair of sparkling beady eyes. The tree shook violently and leaves flew as if a hurricane whirled within the branches. Loud squeaks and squawks indicated an epic battle for blood was taking place amongst the boughs. After a while, the owl fell out of the tree dead. A shadow followed by a long tail scampered down the tree and ran off into the night. I recognized the hooked tail. But why would Ace The Rat be following me? What was Tabby and Bill up to? Should I do as told and deliver the jar to Dorothy Green? Would that solve the mystery? But I'm a cat and perfectly patient. All things are revealed to me sooner or later.

I'm amused by people's treachery and their clumsy attempts of one-up-man-ship. For instance, the Grays who take care of me, they think I don't know what they're doing when they're doing what they do in that big bed of theirs. I also know of her secret affairs with cucumbers. She slices them and puts them under her eyes and in every dish imaginable--including her shrimp salad, which I refuse to eat. Even he complains about the weird cucumber soup. "It looks like a green dick floating in my bowl!" he shouts. I lie on the edge of their bed with my paws folded underneath me like the sphinx watching him grunt and thrust into her for five minutes. He farts loudly, rolls off, and falls fast asleep. She lies next to him for a few minutes with her gown hiked above her white thighs as if there's more to come. Seeing that the candle has burned out, she tips out of the bedroom and goes to the refrigerator and grabs a cucumber. She steals away to the spare bedroom, listens and makes sure his snoring is as regular and loud as the Number Ten bus that rumbles up Tuna Boulevard. The cucumber becomes her everything and she makes love to it like a mad woman. They have different names depending on her moods--*Mel Gibson*, *Justin Timberlake*, *Woody Allen*. Yes, ol' Woody for short. But sometimes she screams out Ellen Degeneres and I'm left to ponder. The woman is out of control with her cucumber. Her toes dig into the blue bedspread until it resembles roiling storm waves. Suddenly the seizure hits her and the only name she can call is God, which she utters for a good three minutes until her breath and voice subside. She then gets up and makes him a cucumber sandwich for his lunch and slides back into bed with the bozo. I wonder if he notices his cucumber sandwiches have a slight fish aroma?

There's another underhanded thing she does. She arrives home from her job after him and goes into the spare bedroom where he never enters. Her Mother died there, cursing to the end of her life. The vixen pretends she's looking for something, calls him in, and points out the rumpled bed. He, of course, blames me until she brings up the point the door is always closed. He stands scratching his head while she screams and accuses him of having another woman in the house. Of course, he begs and swears he's not having an affair. She's not appeased until he buys either flowers or some kind of jeweled bauble the next day as a peace offering.

"Slick bitch," I say to myself. Believe me, I know the wiles of women. I must solve the mystery of this Tabitha Davenport business.

*****

Sometimes a leopard has to change his stripes, and a tiger his spots...Hmm, I gotta lay off this Slim-Fast. What I'm trying to get at is I have to go deep cover to learn more about these shady cats I'm dealing with. No pun intended. I saw my perfect opportunity while perusing the "Meow Meow Gazette." Typically the Meow Meow winds up in the bottom of my litter box. It's nothing but a muckraking rag screaming such headlines *as CANNIBAL TOMS MAKE CAT SOUP*

*FROM KITTENS...CAT MATES WITH ELEPHANT-A CATELEPHANT IS BORN...ELVIS'S CAT LIVES ON THE MOON...MYSTERY CAT CLAIMS TO BE KENNEDY ASSASSIN...*And it goes on. However, something of interest in the want-ads section caught my attention. Of course, those ads are just as lurid. *WANTED: TAIL CURLER...PAYING GOOD MONEY FOR CAT EARS...DONATE YOUR DEAD CAT'S EYES TO MARBLE FACTORY...*But a certain little gem caught my eye: *DISCRETE FRNCH MAID NEED. NQUIRE at CUBBYHOLE ARM ASK FOR DOROTY GREN Apt 411.*

So Dorothy Green needed a maid. What could a cheapskate like her be willing to pay seeing how she was trying to economize on the ad by deleting letters? Or maybe she just couldn't spell. In any case, I needed that job.

Now you're thinking how could my muscular manly self ever get a job as a petite French Maid? A cat has his ways, as many clueless humans will testify. Plus it helps to have gay friends. Sylvester doesn't call himself a hairdresser. He calls himself a "Transformation Engineer." And that's just what I needed, to be transformed. I headed over to his studio after dark. After about ten hours of tucking, duct tape wrapping, and umpteen-hundred wig try-ons, I emerged in the morning light as Brigitte. "Brigeet!" Sylvester proclaimed.

I thought it best not to go home and face those neighborhood hoodlums in Cat Alley. In fact walking anywhere in stiletto heels was out of the question. I felt like a ham or turkey trussed up to be carved for dinner. I hailed a Canary cab. In five minutes, I arrived in front of the Cubbyhole Arms. After arguing with the driver over the fare, I sent him on his way and sauntered up to number Four-one-one. The canary wing in my purse would make a nice snack for later. I rang the doorbell. Dorothy Green answered. A hair curler teetered between her ears. A cigarette dangled from her mouth. Her robe was loose around her bosom. She picked at her teeth with a catfish bone.

"Wat da ya want?"

"I'm here about the position you advertised for in the Meow Meow." I tried to be as dainty and coquettish as possible despite the fact she was blowing smoke in my face. She looked me up and down.

"Come in, I guess. I told that fool to advertise in the New York Times. Ya never knows what's gonna show up at the door from the Meow Meow. Ya look kind of robust for a French Maid."

"I've been told I have a Rubenesque figure."

"Who told ya that?"

"Ruben himself."

"Well honey, take it from me, don't believe everything some lying Tom tells ya. Have a seat."

I sat as daintily on the sofa as possible. I stifled my instinct to raise my tail and give it a good spraying. I noticed a whip and pair of handcuffs lying on the floor. I remembered the scene with Bill, Tabitha, and Dorothy. I cleared my throat and eyed the whip with the hope Dorothy would offer some explanation. She said nothing but perched in an easy chair eying me between puffs of smoke and picks at her teeth.

"Bill wanted someone dainty thing to serve us our breakfast fishcakes. You look like the type who used to work on a lobster trawler. Where have you worked?"

"Only at zee finest hotels in Paree along zee Champs Eleyonce!"

"Hmm." Dorothy seemed less impressed with my French accent than I. Suddenly she screamed at a wall,

"Bill, come out from under the bed and see what the Meow Meow sent you!"

Bill Davenport tipped into the room. His checkered boxers hung low off his backside. He sniffed Dorothy's foot and meowed.

"Not now, you fool. Look at what the Meow Meow sent."

Bill glanced at me. The hair stood up on his back. He bared his teeth.

"Oh-oh," I thought. "He senses I'm a male. My cover is about to be blown." I crossed my legs and purred as softly and sweetly as I could. That seemed to settle him down although his ears stayed back and his eyes glazed like new buttons.

"Oh calm down, Bill. You can't be excited by the likes of that." Dorothy turned to me. "What he really wanted Miss, uh…"

"Brigitte," I squeaked.

Dorothy stared at me. My mind raced to come up with a last name that sounded French. I remembered Diane reading a French magazine. "Brigitte Mademoiselle!" I blinked and tried to blush.

Bill and Dorothy frowned at me. This isn't working I thought to myself. Sylvester had said duct tape could only do so much to hide a muffin tummy and fat ass. As much as I guzzled Slim-Fast I should be skinny as sparrow legs. But Slim-Fast has the opposite effect on me than it does humans. Bill finally spoke up.

"Dorothy and I wanted…"

"Don't put me in this filthy business."

"Well, I wanted and Dorothy was willing to go along with the idea," he nudged her side, "Of a cute little French maid to serve us fishcakes in bed. There's no cooking involved. Just heat them in the oven and serve them while wearing a little French maid's costume."

"Like the one I have on?"

"Well yes, but smaller. That looks like about a size sixteen. We, um, I, was thinking more along the likes of a size one, three at the most."

"What about hiring me to clean? This joint, I mean your lovely domicile looks like it could use a maid's touch."

"Polly Parrot's Maid Service sends in an army of feather dusters on Monday morning. We get good service and an excellent snack to boot," Bill said.

"I see. Perhaps I could serve at your parties."

"How do you know we have parties?"

I winked at the whip and handcuffs to let them know where I was coming from. "I just assumed a debonair and interesting couple like yourselves threw some very exotic parties."

"Well, don't assume," Dorothy snorted and stood. "I'm sorry we won't be able to use you."

I rose from the sofa. I wasn't done. I wanted to see as much of the apartment as possible. "Might I use your *La Salle de Bains?"

"My what?"

"Bathroom."

"I guess so." Dorothy pointed toward the hall. "First door to your left. If you mess it up, you clean it up," she chuckled.

"Of course," I said. As I left them, Bill nibbled at her ear.

Around the corner and out of view, I darted into their bedroom. The room was a mess. The carpets were stained where hairballs had been spat. Empty cans of tuna overflowed the trashcan. The bed sheets were rumpled and stained with the unimaginable. The dresser held a curious collection of pens, toys, balls of yarn, tiny parakeet key chains, and stuffed toy mice. Handcuffs and a pair of leg irons lay tangled across the bed. What really caught my attention was the little fish shaped urn. It was similar to the one Tabitha had given me. I made a note of it and tipped to the bathroom. As my eyes adjusted to the semi-darkness, I was confronted with dozens of those urns in all colors and sizes. I took the smallest one and tucked it in my garter. I wanted to open the medicine cabinet but knew it could be booby-trapped. That vixen owner of mine gets a kick out of putting marbles in hers just to startle curious guests. On the edge of the sink was a card. I picked it up and it read: ACE Detective Services. On the edge of the card was a small spot of blood. "There's a rat at work here." I said to myself.

"Are you okay in there?" Dorothy called from the living room.

I flushed the toilet. "So sorry it took so long. I didn't want to leave a mess," I said scampering back to them.

"Just thought perhaps you had gotten lost. Do you have a card in case we change our minds and decide to use your services after all?"

"Yes, I do." I absently fished in my purse and handed them a card. Instantly when I watched Dorothy's ears spring back, I knew I had made a mistake. I had given them a card from my detective agency. Her claws extended an inch. The tips were curled and red. I sprang for the door, pushed it open with all of my weight, and shimmied up a tree next to their patio. I jumped from branch to branch until I was near the top. When I looked back, Dorothy stood on the patio hissing at Bill and tearing my card to shreds.

Chapter 4 - Plot Thickens

The next day, I heard the garbage can rattling in the alley behind my office. I was sure it was Ace The Rat. I snuck out the cat door and crept toward the trashcans. A stringy black hook shaped tail swept back and forth outside our can's rim. I grabbed the tail in my teeth and clamped down. Whatever was inside let out a gut-wrenching scream. When it leaped, hissing and pawing the air, I recognized the patchy mottled coat and let go of the tail. Sneaky Sam fell back into the pail but quickly scrambled out.

"Man, Catnip, I just wanted some of your sardine crumbs," he said as he sat in my office licking his tail and nibbling on a sardine. I slurped a little bit of Slim-Fast to calm my nerves.

"I saw the stringy hooked tail and assumed you was a rat--a particular rat named Ace," I said.

"Man, word from the streets is that dude's been missing in action for a minute."

"Hmm," I said to myself. I thought about the spot of blood I had seen on his business card. Another piece of the puzzle to solve.

Sneaky Sam looked at his tail. He switched it back and forth and a black string swept across the floor. He made a futile attempt to catch the string, but it eluded him.

"Kids!" he snorted. "Darn kids."

"Your folk's kids?"

"Nah man, neighborhood kids. They caught me asleep under a shade tree and thought it would be funny to tie a dog-shaped balloon to my tail. They then lit a firecracker. That woke me up and put my ass in the wind. When I looked back, there was this balloon dog following me. I thought it was real. Every time I thought it was safe to stop, I'd look back and that dog be looking like he's about ready to tear me a new hole. I'd take off running again. This went on for hours. Folks stopped to take pictures and videos of my distress. I hear I'm all over something called You Tubby..."

"YouTube."

"Whatever. I ran my ass off zigzagging every which way trying to shake that beast with teeth bared at my tail. I saw some low hedges and thought maybe that would be a safe haven. As I dove underneath the balloon popped and I thought for sure, the beast had shot me. I leaped up and hit my head on a thick branch below the bush. When I came to, I swore the black night was hell and a woman passing in a red dress was the devil. A cool breeze blew across my face. I began to recognize some familiar sights. Of course, the balloon is history, but as you can testify by the fact you almost bit my tail off, its remnants are still causing me misery."

"Didn't you feel those delinquents tying the string to your tail?" I asked.

"I was having this dream in which I was standing by a lake with my tail in the water catching fish."

"Have your folks take you to the vet and have her cut the string off."

"Are you crazy? I'd rather die than go back to that Marquis de Sade. Nothing she likes better than probe around your ass while whispering sweet nothings in your ear."

"It's all for the greater good of your health."

"Well, let's see how you feel...Yow! Lord God from heaven!"

Sneaky Sam jumped straight out of his chair. His tail was down and his hair bristled on his back like a porcupine's. Not knowing what was coming next, I too assumed a defensive posture. He hissed and pointed at the two jars on my desk.

"What in God's name are you doing with those?"

"It's just a harmless little jar. You want me to open it?" I pawed at the cork in the mouth of the bottle.

"Don't! Don't!" Sneaky Sam screamed and bolted out the window. The String hanging from his tail got caught in a nail and yanked off. He hollered but kept on going. Tires screeched. I looked out the window in time to see Sneaky Sam tumbling under a Buick Roadmaster. It was not a pretty sight. The Roadmaster was round one. As Sneaky Sam managed to get up on his feet, round two came roaring around the corner. A Mack truck pulling a trailer of "Little Friskies" bore toward Sneaky.

"Oh the irony," I thought to myself. But the truck's driver hit the brakes and stopped a nose from Sneaky Sam's nose. However, the trailer had a mind of its own. It buckled and curved like an accordion before slamming into a tree. Little Friskies spilled from the gash in the trailer's side like confetti. The streets filled with cats. In a word, it was **cat**astrophic.

Sneaky continued across the street oblivious to the pandemonium he had caused. Ah! It was the little jar in my hand that actually caused all hell to break loose. What was it about this jar that had frightened him so? I sat pondering and mulling the rest of the day. Then it hit me. There's a certain rat I need to get to sing like a bird. But first I had to have help catching him--that is if he was still alive. I picked up the phone and dialed a number. The party on the other end of the receiver said Hello, followed by a nauseating hacking. I thought to myself, "Dang, he's puking his guts out." After the hacking, the phone got quiet and a voice calmly stated, "Buttons speaking." Yes, I would need the hairball king to help me set an elaborate trap for Ace the Rat.

****

I've been avoiding that Tabitha dame for a week now. It's crazy to do that to a woman with a purse full of sardines and a body to boot. But I had a big fish to fry, a lot of yarn to untangle, birds to catch. You get my drift?

Buttons sat in my office licking himself. He was a mess of tangled black and white fur. He looked like a zebra. I always wondered why his folks named him Buttons, for he certainly wasn't cute as a button, in any way, shape or form. He stopped and heaved dry air. Oh God, I thought, not here not now. Buttons settled down and licked his paw. He lit a cigarette. The first puff sent him into another coughing frenzy. After a moment, he calmed himself. He licked his tail and took another puff from his cigarette. I offered Buttons a little Slim-Fast. He declined, saying it was bad for his stomach. I wondered how anything could make his stomach any worse than it already was.

"So you think one of my hairballs will catch the Ace fella, huh?"

I wanted to say, "One of your hairballs can trap an elephant." But I calmly nodded.

"Well, just tell me where to do the dirty deed and I will give it all I've got. And baby, I got a lot," Buttons grinned.

I knew Ace hung out near a divvy restaurant call the Trash Bin. But if Buttons spat his famous seafood seasoned hairball near the joint, the smell would empty out the whole place making it harder to trap Ace. Folks didn't go to the Trash Bin to eat. They went there to imbibe the establishment's famous drinks. Their Salmon Blood martinis are to die for. No, I needed to catch Ace closer to home. But if I lured Ace here, these alley-cat hoodlums would get to him trapped in a giant hairball and tear him apart. I thought and thought while Buttons yawned and flicked his tail. A feline walked by. She straddled the fence and carried a kitten in her mouth. Her tunic dress barely covered her honey gold behind. "A loose woman," I said to myself. "Probably some dame from the Cubbyhole Apartments." It hit me. I would ask Buttons to cough up his hairball near the Cubbyhole. That would draw Ace. Once I had him trapped, I had an ingenious way of making him talk. A recording of a snapping rat-trap is mightier than the sword to a blindfolded rat. Buttons thought the cubbyhole idea was good. But he had one reservation. It seems he always winds up in court behind a paternity suit whenever he goes near the Cubbyhole. He owed three felines back kitten support. He has to work in the middle of the day to pay his obligations while most cats are asleep.

"Just wrap it up and hack and go," I told Buttons.

Chapter 5 - A Tail Unravels

Normally pigeons keep a safe distance on the other side of my picture window. A few fools fly into the glass, get up and wobble off as if they've had a couple of bottles of Slim-Fast. But this bird was different. The window was open just enough to trap her fat body. She pushed but could go no further. She stared at me, no doubt wondering what kind of jam she had gotten herself into. I yawned wide, partly out of boredom and partly out of my desire to show her my sharp teeth. Her eyes widened. I could hear her heart beating. I thumped my tail on the floor. I got up and stretched and to consider my options. I could bite her head off, but she might fall out of the window, and wander headless into the clutches of the alley cats, to enjoy her ample breasts and hips. If I left her in the window, those fools I belong to would simply raise the window and shoo her away. In my desire to help, I went outside and nudged her rump until she was safely inside my office. When I slipped back inside through the cat door, she waddled right up to my nose and cooed, "How do?"

"Is it dinnertime yet," I asked sardonically and ironically.

"Feathers would not become you," she answered.

"You've got the nerve of ten Blue Jays," I said lying down and yawning.

"And as many problems as the squirrels, they chase," the pigeon answered.

I loved her wit and decided to entertain her a bit, before we lunched together.

"How can I help you, Miss--?" I paused.
"Pauline Davenport."
"Of the Davenports?"
"Yes."
"How can that be?" I asked looking at her suspiciously. Everyone knows the Davenports are well-heeled cats, a la Bill Davenport the scion of his family's wealth and that wife of his, who wants to divorce him and get half his fortune.
"Our histories go back over a thousand years ago when cats and birds were friends, or, at least, walked amongst each other without fear. During this period of enlightenment, there occurred the matrimony of Sir William Catsenberg Davenport and Lady Jane Beakshire. Soon after, arose a horrible famine that seemed to kill off a lot more birds than cats. It was rumored the cats had cannibalized the birds in order to survive. Feuds were started to avenge deaths. We've been enemies ever since."
The cuckoo clock struck five even though it was noon. I had attempted to have it fixed with the sardines I made off of Tabitha Davenport. But five was as far as she would strike without new springs imported from Germany, the old cockatoo clockmaker told me. I knew he was milking me for more money. You can't milk a milk lover like me. I left him minus his leg and thigh. Now this loaded pigeon Pauline Davenport walks into my life. Cans of sardines rained in front of my eyes. I knew the Cat Davenports were in films and cheap eateries. I inquired as slyly as I could about Pauline's source of wealth.
"The union Davenport-Beakshire was a union made in hell. Those dirty cats used the guts of sparrows executed for petty crimes to catch fish. They, in turn, made a fortune selling fish to the seagulls. All of this

was before seagulls could fly well enough to trust themselves over water. My ancestors the pigeons were in collusion with the cats. We fed the sparrows false information of breadcrumb locations. When the sparrows arrived at the trap, they were accused of loitering or pecking without a license and executed on the spot. It became a cat eat bird world then and continues to this day. We own all of the popcorn concessions located in the Davenport movie houses. Sparrows fattened on our popcorn wind up in the cat restaurants the Davenports control and into the bellies of cats. Cats, in turn, make a sport of hunting us down. It's a dog eat dog world."

"Sounds like a cat and pigeon eat sparrow world," I said. I thought of the Cinema 80 over on Flounder Avenue. They threw out enough stale popcorn to feed half the birds in the city. On any night, the parking lot, telephone poles, and dumpsters drew thousands of birds. How many suspected they were unwittingly being fattened up for the likes of me and my kind? I burped.

"I was supposed to meet a friend at the Owl and Pussycat. He didn't show up," Pauline continued.

I looked at her beady eyes and beak nose. What an ugly dame, I thought. I would have stood her up too. The Grays had had fish last night. They left the grease filled pan on top of the stove. I imagined Pauline swimming in a pan of hot grease. If only I knew how to turn the darn stove on. As I sat staring at Pauline, her eyes suddenly glazed over. She became still as if hypnotized.

"Dang, I gotta stop doing that," I said to myself. I didn't mean to charm this chick. This golden pigeon was loaded with sardines. I needed her alive. I waved my paw in front of Pauline's face to break her out of her trance. Her beak opened, and she vomited the vile contents of her stomach.

Bits of yellowed popcorn, a scrap of pink confetti from a noisemaker, the green head of a fly, and five small gemstones littered my floor. I studied the gems. They were fake. Probably picked out of some costume jewelry that had been tossed in the trash. She probably used them to help her gizzard grind up the rest of the junk she ate. But what really got to me was the piece of long skinny black tail with a white tip. This was unmistakably the tail of Ace the Rat. Pauline Davenport lay on the floor with her feet in the air. I got up and nosed around her body and pushed her over onto her side. She had a small hole in the back of her head, the size of a BB. I ran to the opened window just in time to hear tires squealing and the butt end of a red Jaguar whipping around the corner.

"My God," I thought. "Why did the richest pigeon in town have to pick my place to get knocked off?"

I called Buttons. "Say, forget about that hairball business. Ace, the rat, got trapped in the belly of a bird."

"I would like to meet that bird," Buttons said.

"Too late. She's dead meat." I hung up the phone.

I opened my cat door and looked about. Not a soul in sight. I nosed Pauline's body out my door and down the sidewalk. I growled and ran back into my office. The alley cat hoodlums stuck their noses out from the hedges. They saw Pauline's body and pounced on it like a pride of Hyenas. In a moment, all that was left of Pauline was a single feather floating upward as if trying to reach the blue skies. I could have waited for that Diane to arrive home and sweep Pauline up with a broom and dustpan, but she always scolds me for killing the "little birdies." Heck, I'm a man, a darn tomcat at that. What does she expect me to do, invite them to tea? I picked up the phone and dialed Tabitha Davenport's number.

"I can't talk right now. I think Bill is dead," she whispered and hung up the phone. I wondered who was in that Jaguar.

****

Three weeks later, the richest feline in the world sat on my desk. Her Rolls Royce Silver Shadow was parked at my door. Tabitha Davenport clad in black mink and emeralds filed her nails as I read sections of the Ace The Rat's diary. Her Hermes bag bulged with sardines.

*****

Jan 1, 2012, Beginning the year as usual, down on my luck. Reduced to eating crap that drunks hurl from their guts.

Jan 5, 2012, Met a rich dame named Tabitha in Snakes all night eatery. Tabitha woman is loaded. She was there with her hubby and another dame dressed in gray coat, leotards and boots. Tabitha winked at me. I slipped her my card as we passed each other on our way to the litter box.

Jan 6, 2012, Met Tabitha at my office. She was distraught. Husband cheats on her. He scratches her and bites her tail.

Jan 9, 2012, Can bearly sleep thinking of Tabitha's womany charms. Oh how she plays with my soul!

Jan 10, buys suite from Parson's pawn shop. Need to improve my appeerance.

Jan 11, 2012, Tabitha rages and curses the day she met sex fiend hubby. Tabitha will attempt to enlist a stool pigeon to help us in our scheme to get rid of the bastard and his lover Dorthy. Prenuptial agreement limits her alimony to ten sardines a month—hardly enough to live on.

Jan 12, Visit with Mother went well after I bought her booze and gave her a couple of sardines. Tabitha keeps my pockets full. But I'm a rat at heart. Can't stay away from garbage.

Jan 15, Tabitha chooses that never-do-well Dick, Catnip of the Catnip Gray Detective Agency. Bill's death must appear accidental. Triple Indemnity on the Ins policy

Feb 13, She gives Catnip vial of deadly Catnip1090 and sends him on a mission to visit the Gray woman's apt at the cubbyhole. My job is to make sure gas gets piped into the place after the aroma knocks them out. They death will be blamed on the gas leek.

Feb 22, I observe our stoolie spying in the Dorthy Gray Feline's apt window instead of making the delivery. I suggest to Tabitha we bump him off. He was too curious. She replied she had bigger fish to fry. I dont know what she mean.

Tabitha sighed. "This is about as exciting as a report on flea collars. What's the point of all of this? Is this the only comfort you can offer a young widow?" She batted her lashes.

I ignored her and continued reading even as the overpowering aroma of her cologne, White Diamond Fish Oil and those sardines made my nostrils flare.

March 15, Bill Davenport's cousin Pauline gets wind of Tabitha's scheme to take control of the Davenport umpire. Threatens to squawk to the cops. Tabitha says she has a plan to take care of Pauline. We have to move quickly. Tabitha says she can't wait to lay in my arms as my wife.

April 1, I dress like a brown poodle Delivery guy from PUPS and deliver vial of poisonous catnip to Bill and Dorothy's love nest. The package is labeled Shark Aphrodisiac. Turns out for them to be the most deadly April Fool's joke ever. They die within minutes of opening the jar and inhaling the contents

April 40th, Tabitha takes control of Davenport Industries. She dumps me. I'm delirious with heartbreak. She used me! All I have are her pictures of us and the recording her of voice whispering sweet nothings in my ear.

May 1. I get a strange call from the pigeon Pauline Davenport's cellphone asking to meet with me at the Owl and Pussycat Lounge. Her voice is hoarse. She says she has a touch of bird flu, but is okay. She wants to plot revenge on Tabitha. I question her choice for the meetup. She said Tabitha would be there and buy drinks. I take pellet gun.

That was the last entry in Ace's diary. I put one and six together and came up with seven ninety-nine. Well math has never been my favorite subject. But I surmise

Ace went to the Owl and Pussycat to meet with Pauline, only Pauline wasn't there. Or by the time she arrived, the owls had torn him to shreds. She being a silly pigeon mistook the tail for a worm. Someone followed her to my place and shot her in the head with a BB gun. But, "Who, who, who," quoth the owl. It could be none other than Tabitha Davenport. But I had called her right after I saw the Jaguar speeding away. Who shot Pauline Davenport?

"So what's the point of this filibuster, Mr. Catnip?" Tabitha lifted and groomed the tip of her tail. Her tongue darted seductively from her small mouth.

"The point is someone needs to go to jail."

"Go to jail for what? What court in cat land will convict me based on the deranged musings entered in a mouse's diary? It's obviously a work of fiction. Bill and that Dorothy woman's death was an accident. You want to know who shot Pauline Davenport?"

I nodded my head.

"My chauffeur did it."

"You chauffeur?"

"Yes. The old homing pigeon was madly in love with her. But she wouldn't give him the time of day. She insulted him constantly. The straw that broke that pigeon's back was the day she and the young sparrow she was dating shit all over the windshield of the freshly washed car. He seethed with rage and vowed to kill her. I tried to calm him down, even threatened to eat him. Nothing worked."

I had figured she would come up with a brazen tail, or tale. That's why I had had Sneaky Sam fix me up with a wire. I wanted that dame to convict herself.

"Are you denying you had anything to do with your husband's death, his paramour's death, and the death of his closest relative?" There was feedback from the recorder and a sudden squeal coming from under my coat made me wince. I tried to play it off like a bad case of gas. Tabitha looked at me and smiled. She excused herself to use my restroom and lingered for a while. I knew the place was windowless but was she attempting a cowardly act of hara-kiri? I knew Diane's fishnet pantyhose were slung over the shower curtains. I was worried.

Tabitha emerged from the bathroom pushing a large spool of toilet paper across the floor. She wore nothing but her boots. All decorum and sensibilities were cast aside. My buttons were pushed. I immediately pounced on the roll and it scooted across the floor. Tabitha leaped after it. We frolicked in the fluffy white sheets. I untangled myself and watched Tabitha bat and roll in the paper until she mummified herself in scented softness.

"I seem to be your prisoner Mr. Catnip. What will you do with me?" She twitched her tail seductively.

It wasn't even mating season, but I was driven to a frenzy. I began to nibble the end of her tail. She moaned seductively. I pulled her tail and she arched her back. I mounted her and nibbled at her ears.

"If it were mating season, the things I could do to you," I whispered in her ear.

"I have a little something to get you in the mood." She nodded toward her Hermes bag. I opened it and took out a small fish vial. She sensed my hesitation. "Open it, Mr. Catnip. It's harmless."

I opened the vial and it released an odor of musk that drives us male cats wild. I tore away the tissue swaddling Tabitha's shapely frame. I squeezed the back of her neck. She moaned and growled low. I began to mew loudly and moan. I was almost at the point of no return. I felt my member easing toward her soft flesh.

"What kind of detective doesn't own a pair of handcuffs?"

I caught her drift. I retrieved the cuffs and a silk scarf I used as a blindfold. I handcuffed her around the base of a stout table leg. I mounted her again and squeezed her neck.

"Oh Catnip, she moaned. The next minute, she hissed and growled as if she didn't want me. She bit my ear but purred with desire and lust. Then it was my turn to take charge. I licked between her ears until she was a bundle of mewing softness. My lips nuzzled the soft flesh around her neck. She mewed, hissed, and spit at me. Then she licked my face seductively. My member could no longer control itself. It shot into her. She yelped and bolted upright as far as the cuffs allowed her. She rolled on her belly and shook herself. The deed was complete. I had had my way with Tabitha Davenport.

"Now about that diary, Mr. Catnip," Tabitha said stroking my chest as we lay on the floor, "It would make a fine batch of cat litter—a fitting tribute for the horrible rat who killed my husband in a jealous rage."

I hesitated. The diary was enough to send Tabitha to prison for life, or maybe even to the gas chamber. There were many entries and more sordid details of her and Ace's plots to do away with Bill Davenport—poison his tuna, lure him to an aquarium filled with piranha fish, sprinkle the next door Doberman's doggy dish with catnip to lure poor Bill into the vicious animal's jaws. Their morbid imaginations knew no bounds. Yet I hesitated spellbound by Tabitha's charms. She stroked me behind my ears until I purred in ecstasy. Her feline charms won. I handed her the gnawed diary. I watched her dress. She went into her Hermes bag and tossed one hundred sardines on the bed. She then placed the diary inside.

“You’re a good boy, Mr. Catnip--a very good boy. Buy yourself a new suit. A feline of my caliber will need a well-dressed tom to escort her about town. I will call on you again after my period of mourning is over.”

I sipped from a saucer of catnip and watched Tabitha’s hips sway as she walked toward her Rolls Royce. I helped a feline get away with murder. Did I like it? I picked up one of the sardines and sniffed its rich aroma. That answered my question.

Chapter 6 – Cuckold

"What a fool you are, Mr. Gray. What a fool."

Tabitha Davenport sat next to me wearing my handcuffs. We were in her Rolls Royce. A cop car followed and one led the way to the city jail. "I would have made you a very rich man. But, you tricked me for thirty pieces of sardines—bits and pieces. "

"I had nothing to do with that Tabitha."

"Of course you and that snake had nothing to do with betraying me."

"Tabitha, I didn't know what Sneaky Sam was up to. I promise."

Tabitha sighed and looked out the window. "The last time I will see the outside world, its beauty and its ugliness." She looked at me. I looked off, but held onto to her handcuffed paw. The chain of events that led to this moment, were swift and ugly like a stream full of dead salmon.

I thought back on the night, me and Sneaky Sam searched Ace the Rat's room. Ace lived in a hole-in-a-wall behind the refrigerator in a filthy kitchen. A family named Swunk owned the joint. You could smell the Swunks and their kids from a mile away. One of the mangy alley cays belonged to them. Sneaky and me put our paws to our noses as we entered the hole. Sneaky lapped some spilled milk that had curdled on the floor. I chewed a roach or two. They tasted like bacon. Evidently they had been swimming in grease. Tacked on the wall was a picture of Tabitha, he had ripped from the Meow Meow's Society Column. In fits of hunger or anger, he had gnawed the picture and had drawn hearts as daggers all over it. Fish bones, dog turds, and used diapers littered the floor. An assortment of sticks and planks served as furniture. His bed was a pile of rags and torn newspapers. We swiped at the bed with our paws until we turned it over and found the diary stained with piss, blood, and tears.

As I read the sordid epistle, I could see Tabitha was leading him on. *"She yanked my tail playfully ... She tossed me in the air ... She bit my ear ..."* Poor rat, mistaking her signs of wanting to eat him as love. I looked at Tabitha's spoiled picture. Ace was a rat in the throes of passion. I imagined him twisting under the ravishing emotions of love and hate tormenting his soul. He was no fool, yet he was a fool for love. I read the incriminating passages that chronicled Tabitha's role in having her husband bumped off. I sighed and out the diary in my pocket. What wretchedness!

Sam and I searched through boxes. We found a pellet pistol. I sniffed it and knew it had recently been fired. No doubt this was the gun that had killed Pauline Davenport. I'd have it sent to the crime lab, so the boys in red could dust it for prints. Hmm, don't all cops wear red? Anyway, Sneaky and I searched other boxes for those photos and voice recordings Ace had alluded to. Nothing, so I thought. I saw Sneaky rifling through another box in Ace's closet. When I approached, he shoved it in the back.

"Nothing here, Catnip except his Ratboy Magazine collection."

If you've never seen Ratboy, pray you go blind before you do. It showcases the most hideous she-rats on the planet. Creatures bearing their teeth, long noses, beady eyes, and tails wrapped seductively around their bodies, barely covering their tiny nipples. It once featured *Miss September Rat* floating in a toilet. Ugh! I thanked Sneaky Sam for sparing me. We searched a few more spots until the overpowering stench of the place made my eyes water. I gave Sam the pellet gun to turn over to the cops. That night I drowned my sorrows and nursed my disgust with two saucers of Slim-Fast. Bella sung a song that echoed my feelings:

Use me, baby
Use me until you
Use me up,
Drink me dry
Until I cry.
Your sinful sinning ways
Make me wanta cry cry cry

The next day I read the Meow Meow headlines as the Grays changed my litter box:

DAVENPORT FAMILY OFFERS $10,000 SARDINES FOR BILL's KILLER!

A funny feeling swept over my fur. I thought about the box Sneaky Sam had abruptly pushed away when I approached. When I went back later that night to look for the box, it had vanished. I knew I had been double-crossed. The next morning:

CAT RATS ON CAT! DAVENPORT FELINE JAILED!

The Meow Meow printed a whole page of pictures showing Tabitha and Ace frolicking in hole in the wall dives around town. They printed snippets from the audio Ace had recorded of Tabitha plotting her husband's murder. The cops dressed as trash collectors raided my house before I could destroy the diary.

"This old thing," Diane Gray asked the cop with a banana peel hanging out of shoe. "I think he drug it home from someone's garbage can last night. Sure you can have it."

I felt like a slug, tasty but slimy. Cats all over the world were having a field mouse day. I felt like a clod in a litter box. But, none of this consoled Tabitha as we rode to the jail. I thought back on that day we frolicked with the toilet tissue.

"You've made me a very happy man, Tabitha. A very happy man." I stroked her hand.

"Your happiness is my misfortune. I trusted you. I had millions of sardines. Yet you and your cohort betrayed me for such a tiny sum. It's my love for you that allows me to let you ride in the car with me on my way to my doom."

"I never betrayed you and I will never forget you," I said.

She turned and looked out the window. Her jewels sparkled as News cameras flashed and Doves cooed into their microphones, the Downfall of Tabitha Davenport. It took all of her fortune to keep her from getting the gas chamber.

Epilogue

Diane's husband finally put a video camera in the spare bedroom. He had sought to prove that it was I breaking into the bedroom and messing up the covers. To his surprise, he discovered his wife's infidelities with cucumbers. They had a terrible fuss of course.

"If you were more of a man, I wouldn't have to resort to fruits and vegetables for satisfaction."

"Fruits? You've been getting it on with fruits behind my back?"

"Yes I have. Bananas and big black plantains! Big thick black ones. Oh how I love to taste their sweetness. You, you're just a little pink shrimp! You'll never be any match for a black banana!"

He slapped her and she fell to her knees and groveled at his feet. Now he punishes Diane with a nightly spanking as he works her nether regions over with a cucumber or a plantain. Gone are the days, he brings flowers and jewels. In fact they've pawned the jewelry to buy an assortment of dildos and other sex toys. They even go shopping together for fruits and veggies. I'll never understand these people, but the truth set him free.

Post Epilogue – Two Months Later

The postman rang twice one Saturday. He was an old retired Cardinal, who was forced to make ends meet by delivering mail. He had been defrocked for some indelicate situation with the Church's ceramic cherubs. The Cardinal pushed open the mail slot to drop some letters through. I caught his wing and thought of pulling him into the house. He must be tired, I reasoned and would have enjoyed taking a load off, and perhaps even related to me stories of intrigue at the Vatican. Of course, he protested loudly. The Grays were in the spare bedroom playing with their new video camera. I didn't want her or him running into the room, so I let the Cardinal go after he deposited his mail. I was preparing to go out for the evening with a new dame I had met and didn't relish being put on any kind of punishment. Me having a cardinal with relish would have put me on lockdown in the kitchen for a week. My new girl Samantha is burnt orange and full of fire. The neighborhood hoodlums don't even mess with her after she sent one tumbling between the wheels of an armored car. He survived minus a left foot and an eye.

I retrieved the epistle. It was stamped Catacombs State Prison: Prisoner 789945901. I didn't have to open it to know whom it was from. Tabitha had drawn a teardrop and a heart on the envelope with a black crayon. I ate a crayon once. It was the most tasteless thing outside of a tuna can label you can imagine. Anyhow, the letter read:

Dear Mr. Catnip Gray:

I hope this letter finds you well, happy and wise. I have adjusted well in here. I'm teaching foreign languages--Duck, Goose, and French Hen. It's all useless folly since none of us are going to the exotic places where those languages are spoken. But it gives me something to do. Perhaps, my children—all six of them, shall one day have the privilege of world travel. Yes, children! I'm in a very pregnant condition right now, thanks to you, Mr. Gray. You certainly can't deny paternity, Mr. Catnip. You were very loud and vocal. I remember the window being open giving the entire neighborhood an earful of our carrying on. Those wretched hood hoodlums high-fived each other and whistled catcalls at me as I walked to my car. I was so humiliated, but yet happy that I had given the tom I desired all of my love. Witnesses plus the DNA tests will be proof of your paternity. They belong to no other tomcat. The Courts and my lawyers have stripped me of every asset I ever owned. I am a ward of the state and so are my soon to be born kittens. I trust you saved some of those sardines I gave you and the ones you received for being a Judas. The state demands that fathers meet their obligations. Expect a visit from each appointed attorney for each of my kittens. Yes, that may be more of a bother and expense for you. But each Kitten is unique. The judge being a somewhat doltish goose agreed to assign a court-appointed attorney to each kitty. You'll have to pay court costs and each of those lawyers for a case you can't win. Those attorneys are sharks. They'll squeeze you for every penny. Just imagine your kitten support bill. My mother will raise them, and I'll demand they have the finest of everything. So see you in court six times next month. Stock up on your Slim-Fast. You'll be in my claws a very long time, my Dear Catnip.

I suddenly felt nauseated. A hairball rumbled in my stomach.

###

*salle de bain (French for bathroom)

About the Author

Charles Harvey loves writing about offbeat characters.

Excerpt from:

The Holey Sweets Underwear Manufacturing Company

Chapter 1

Edna Glaspey slammed her arms like two fat hams onto the newspaper. She took a pencil in her right hand and began circling ads. Her circles were thick like mascara. Jericho, her grandson, had suggested she use a computer to hunt for a job. But Edna would have none of that. No beeping little box full of blue writing and flashing pictures lead to anything solid, Edna reasoned. "A newspaper is solid," Edna said to Jericho as he lapped coffee out of a saucer. "Solid as the pages in the Bible."

The first job she encountered as she squinted at the paper through her turtle colored reading glasses was for a hair stylist at Mabel Marley's Hair Emporium. "Shit I wouldn't work for that witch if she was the only hair stylist in town."

"Um Mah Mah, she is the only licensed beautician."

"Nah she ain't. Beulah's got a license. And she do dead colored people's hair, and she don't hire no sissy in her place."

"Can't nobody fit in that nook in her garage but her. Her paper's done expired. That's why she only do hair after five o'clock, and her little bitty sign say '*Air Fixing'* instead of Hair Fixing. She trying to throw off the state inspectors."

"Well, she do my hair just right.'

"Um, I reckon."

"You don't know nothing about women's hair."

"What you need a job for anyhow? You can get on Social Security."

"Social Security this month and dead the next month."

"That's it, Mah Mah! You can do something at Clyde's. His business done picked up since that bullet train started coming through. Just last week it killed a chicken farmer and his wife. Spared all the chickens they was hauling."

"The hoot with you boy! I ain't working in no darn Funeral Home. Darn buzzards flying around there big as eagles."

"Them buzzards don't know dead peoples in there. Whenever I visit, it smells spicy like your ginger cakes. Don't smell like nothing dead to me. I think them buzzards flyin' around 'cause of Banyon's ol' meatpacking plant."

"You get you a job at Clyde's."

"I'm scared of dead peoples."

"And what you think about me?" Edna looked up at her grandson. "And don't be comparing the smell of my ginger cakes to any smell at Clyde's."

"I ain't saying they smell the same."

"Still, don't be mentioning them in the same breath with Clyde's."

"Mah Mah, you said you took typing in High school, and you knows how to sew."

"Dead folks don't need no letters typed and no clothes made."

"I heard they sews their lips together to keep their mouths from popping open grinning at folks like chess cats." Jericho bared his teeth at Edna and got in her face."

"You get outta my face before I take a switch to you, boy."

He got up and walked around the room zombielike--teeth clenched and hands outstretched.

"You stop that dead walking in my kitchen or else I ain't cooking no butter biscuits tonight."

Jericho sat down and slurped his coffee. While Edna had her nose stuck in the paper, he sneaked behind her and pretended to bite her neck. Edna swatted at his nose and hollered for him stop or else.

After a couple more circles, she threw her pencil down and took a sip of coffee.

"Them darn health nuts."

"I feel you, Mah Mah. Why folks from way up in Dallas come down here and meddle in Butler's Butte's business? Talking about rank sausages."

"All they had to do was boil 'em in a stock pot full of salt water with just a little half-teaspoon of bleach. That would have cured the rankness."

"And wouldn't mess up the flavor."

"Nah it wouldn't. Them things had so much pecan wood smoke in them, you could belch a week later and still taste the smoke in your mouth."

"Sure could," Jericho licked his lips.

"But nah, just because a few so-called big shots up there in Dallas got sick, here they come all swooping down on Butler's Butte and Banyon's Meat Packing like we had Osama Ben Laden hidin' out in here. Got the news cameras all up in Mrs. Banyon's face—You know I never thought she was as old as she was. That camera showed all kind of lines and cracks in her jaws. Darn news folks closed down the biggest job around here."

"Mr. Banyon almost went to jail--his poor old trucks. Now sometimes they did break down between here and Dallas and the refrigerators went dead on 'em a lot."

"That don't mean he was being negligible or malicious intentionally," Edna frowned.

"Well, I kept telling him about those trucks. You know I worked on 'em every Saturday evening. You can only keep a truck running for so long. Even if it is a International Harvester," Jericho said with a bit of smugness.

Edna looked up at the star shaped light fixture on her kitchen's ceiling. "You know, Jericho I bet ol' Brown had something to do with some of that negative publicity. He didn't say one word in defense of Banyon's."

"Not a peep. And he the Mayor. He supposed to fight for Butler's Butte."

"And now they bring the Bullet Train from Houston to Dallas through here after Banyon's closed down. Something funny going on. They trying to declare Banyon's land a hazard site and take it away from him. What kind of fighting for your citizens is that?"

"Maybe they want to build a mall on that land."

"A mall?" Edna screeched. "Who gonna shop in it? Ain't enough of us to fill up Piggly Wiggly on Saturday afternoon. A mall," Edna chortled.

"Well if you add Ruby..."

"Ruby is smaller and poorer than we are. Nah. Ain't no mall going on that land. Now I wonder why Brown's son was down here from Washington DC. What he do up there in the capitol?"

"Some kind of Lobby work."

"Now you stone crazy. That *Harva* educated boy ain't cleaning up no lobby."

"I don't know, Mah Mah. If we had a computer we could look him up on Goo Goo."

"Just what in the name of Jesus is that?"

"A thing people go into on the computer when they need to get somewhere."

"Go into the computer to get somewhere?" Edna frowned.

"Aw Mah Mah. I don't know exactly. Solomon says it for news, weather, sports, and a whole lot of stuff. If there was a computer in this house, I'd know more about it."

Edna leveled her eyes at her grandson. "Ain't no computer comin' up in here. Rev. Boyd says it's all kinds of sins in them boxes. He gave a big sermon on homosexuals last Sunday. Speaking of, you better quit hanging around that sissy Solomon. Folk's going to be saying funny things about you."

"Aw nah, they won't. Everybody know me and Sheila is tight."

"Y'all ain't too tight. You ain't married her."

"How we going to get married and I ain't got no job? Ain't we talking about how Banyon's done closed down?"

"You had plenty time to marry her before Banyon's got shut down."

"She got to agree to it too. You know she taking care of her sick mama."

"A woman that take care of her mama got plenty room in her heart for a man."

"I ain't moving in no sick-house."

"I'd rather move in there than be always hanging around that sissy. Don't let me have to read Leviticus to you."

"You ain't reading nothing to me, Mah Mah. Not a thing."

Jericho grabbed his cap off the nail in the doorjamb and stalked out the house.

"Don't let me read Leviticus," Edna shouted at the screeching tires as his truck screamed out of the driveway. "Lord, don't let me read Leviticus in this house," she said to herself as her eyes slowly scanned the column of Help Wanted ads. "Lord, maybe I should let you pick me out a job." She closed her eyes and traced her finger carefully along the paper once, then twice just in case it landed on Mable Marley's ad. Then she traced it some more. She opened her eyes, and her finger had stopped on a tiny peculiar reading ad:

Holey Sweets Underwear Manufacturing
Needs Seamstresses. Please send Resume
To: hr@holeysweets.com

Edna looked at the address and thought it seemed odd. What was she supposed to resume and what kind of address didn't have no street number? She would have to ask Jericho about that when he got back from either Sheila's or Solomon's. *"I wonder if it's some kind of religious concern?"* Edna asked herself. *"Or maybe they mean Holly, and it's got to do with Christmas. Could be a fruitcake operation. But nah, it says underwear. I wonder if Peg or Shawna heard anything about this? Needs seamstress. Now if there is one thing I can do, it is sew. I can whip out a house dress in a day and a Sunday dress in two."* Edna circled her index finger around the advertisement as she sat thinking.

****

People often told Edna she had been wasting her talent at Banyon's stuffing pig entrails with questionable hog parts and things that weren't part of the hog. The only outlet for the display of her sewing talent was her church choir, River Valley Baptist/Butler's Butte Pentecostal Church. She also sewed wedding gowns. Edna belonged to the Baptist side of the slash. The two denominations alternated Sundays and every other Wednesday for worship and choir rehearsal. The Baptists sold fish dinners on Fridays while the Pentecostals sold barbecue dinners on Saturday. For the most part, this arrangement worked out pretty well, unless there was a funeral on Saturday or Christmas fell on a Sunday. Sunday Christmas' was always a bone of contention since both congregations felt they needed to welcome the Lord into the world as early as possible. The Reverend Silas Boyd and Elder-Overseer-Bishop-Prophetess Laura Mae Waters tossed a coin. Before that coin toss, they pulled straws to decide who would be heads and who would be tails. Bishop-Prophetess Laura May always drew the larger straw and chose heads. But tails always won, and the Pentecostals didn't get to hold their Christmas service until almost nighttime. "Lord's been here almost a whole day and we just now getting a chance to celebrate," the Pentecostals groused. If the coin toss couldn't decide the outcome of who could use the Church, the Sheriff settled the matter by threatening to throw Silas Boyd in jail. Sheriff Patton just happened to be Elder-Overseer-Bishop-Prophetess Laura Mae Waters' cousin. Okay, enough of that historical digression.

Edna's blazing blue choir robes could be seen way up in Heaven and was probably blinding the devil himself, folks often remarked. She had spent almost a year turning a remnant roll of sky-blue "sateen" fabric into garments holy enough for the River Valley Baptist Choir. The cloth rolled off of an eighteen-wheeler that hit a bump in the middle of Highway 777. Edna just happened to be driving behind the truck as the roll of material bounced toward her like a huge spool of blue thread. She had her car towed to Banyons' so Jericho could work on replacing the bashed front-end, and had the fabric towed home to her carport. She then ordered two Crisco sized tubs of red sequins and the same quantity of dazzling white sequins. Edna sat all summer underneath the shed with her Singer Sew-A-Matic humming like a wasp's nest. The red sequins formed the initials RVB on the backside of the robes, and the white ones were supposed to be a treble clef over the heart. But folks remarked that her treble clef looked more like a J. Edna not wanting to be outdone by this mishap convinced the choir director Velma Trueblood to adopt the motto "*Singing in the Key of Jesus*." Thus, the J looking musical note was saved in the name of Jesus.

Now there was a little incident with the red blazers she made for the Elks Club men. People would have joined just for the coats, except every member of the Elks Club died after getting sick on a cruise ship that went to the Bahamas and got stuck there for two days. It took about three months for all fifteen of those Elks men to die. But dead is dead no matter how long it takes. Doctors called it *Legion Airs* or something like that.

"And to think how close I came to joining the Elks, Mah Mah," Jericho said as they drove home from burying the last Elk. "I had filled out the application, and you had taken the measurements for my blazer. It almost became my shroud."

"Yep very close--almost as close as you been to marrying Sheila." Edna glanced over the seat and winked at Sheila, who glared at the back of Jericho's high domed bald head. Jericho gunned the motor.

For a while, there was a rumor that there had been Red Dye No. 2 in the fabric that Edna had used to make the jackets, and that was what killed the men. But just as that rumor was about to catch fire and destroy Edna's sewing reputation, The Windstar Phone Company dug some trenches and gave the town Cable TV. *The Discovery Channel* just happened to be running a series called "WHATS KILLING THE RED ELKS?" In an autopsy scene, a Doctor held up a piece of the liver from one of the Elks. He pointed to mottled purple blemishes and used a whole bunch of scientific words and said stuff like, "And a cultured pathology of the left region shows striated variations of the liver…" People in Butler's Butte turned their television sets off and just quietly went about their business. Not a peep was mentioned anymore about Edna, The Elks, or Legion Airs. Good country people are satisfied with, "God had a hand in it."

Edna also stopped making wedding gowns. Now she didn't stop making them because they made anyone sick. But in my opinion, most wedding gowns are downright silly looking. They remind me of a Christmas pageant with all them folds of fabric and veils. All they need is a one of them aluminum foil halos that folks attach to their foreheads pretending to be angels and you can't tell a wedding from a Christmas play. Well, Edna made a wedding dress for Mayor Brown's middle Daughter—the one who has the personality disorder that makes her deliberately try to get stung by bees if she don't take her psychiatrist medicine. They said Brown actually gave the groom--who was a bit slow himself graduating out of high school in Dallas at almost 21--a used Lincoln Town Car, five hundred dollars, plus arranged for him to work at Clyde's Mortuary. The job at Clyde's didn't last long because that boy was, as Clyde put it delicately, "acting peculiar" around the dead women. So anyways Edna made Brianna's gown out of something called cotton candy silk with yellowish lace zigzagging all over it. It was the talk of the town. Folks said it reminded them of a lightning storm. However, people's reaction to things can lead to some odd requests. Women started coming to Edna not for wedding dresses, but for shrouds for themselves to be buried in at some future date.

Edna gave it a try. She made one lavender tunic looking shroud and decided to try it on just before Jericho got off from work. She laid down in that gown on her neatly made up bed, folded her big arms across her chest just like she was a dead woman, and before you know it, she was fast asleep. Jericho came home and saw his grandmother laid out and went to whooping and hollering, he almost scared Edna to death. She jumped off the bed and scared him back to death. And it didn't help matters for her to be running towards him trying to calm him down. He thought for sure, he was being chased by a dead woman. It took the sheriff and the ambulance crew to get them two calmed down. Edna decided she had enough of making shrouds and wedding gowns. The only wedding dress she swore to make was one for Sheila to marry Jericho in. She did make one last shroud for herself to be buried in, hopefully not until she saw Jericho married off or after the year 2020--whichever came first.

****

Yep, Edna knew she was a first-class seamstress, but she sat puzzled as the Saturday sky turned purple, over what Holey Sweets Underwear was all about. Her calls to Peg and Shawna were a waste of time. All them girls could offer was just a whole bunch of country talk about buttermilk pies and Bingo.

"Well," Edna said after she had hung up the phone from Shawna, "I guess I got to go see Blind Pudding," she sighed as raindrops clattered like marbles against the kitchen window.

Connect With Harvey

Other Works

Four Crazy Short Stories
Odd Voices in Love

Twitter
https://twitter.com/CharlesHarvey99
Facebook
https://www.facebook.com/Wes-Writers-Publishers-200150716671422/

Web
Charlesharveyauthor.com

Instagram
https://www.instagram.com/charlesharveyauthor/

The Publisher and Authors from Wes Writers & Publishers strive to bring you the best in fiction and poetry. We support many fine author/brands and diverse fiction genres. We strive for excellence. A better reading experience won't happen without your valuable input. That's why reviews are so helpful. Please take the time and leave a review. We also want to stay in touch with you. The best way to do so is to join our mailing list. By joining, you will get excerpts from our upcoming titles and other

important information about books and publishing. Please subscribe to the mailing list. Thank you.

Made in the USA
Coppell, TX
09 January 2021

47846118R00042